BAD
BUNNIES

Sandra is scared of bunny rabbits.
She's terrified of their
SCARY little bunny faces and
their long NASTY bunny ears and their
EVIL little bunny eyes. So what
is Sandra to do when she finds herself
at the Petting Zoo with a big BAD
bunny snuggling up to her?

MORE BITES TO SINK YOUR TEETH INTO!

THE GUTLESS GLADIATOR
Margaret Clark
Illustrated by Terry Denton

LET IT RIP!
Archimede Fusillo
Illustrated by Stephen Michael King

LUKE AND LULU
Bruce Davis
Illustrated by Chantal Stewart

MISS WOLF AND THE PORKERS
Bill Condon
Illustrated by Caroline Magerl

BAD BUNNIES

SO CUTE, THEY'RE SCARY!

Danny Katz
Illustrated by Mitch Vane

RUNNING PRESS
KIDS
PHILADELPHIA·LONDON

**To my father: a wise man, a rock lover,
a bunny helper—D.K.**

For my sister Becky and her bunnies—M.V.

First published by Penguin Group (Australia),
a division of Pearson Australia Group Pty Ltd, 2006

Printed in China

9   8   7   6   5   4   3   2   1
Digit on the right indicates the number of this printing

Library of Congress Control Number: 2006929395
ISBN-13: 978-0-7624-2924-0
ISBN-10: 0-7624-2924-0

Original design by George Dale and Ruth Grüner,
Penguin Group (Australia).
Additional design for this edition by Frances J. Soo Ping Chow

Typography: New Century School Book
This book may be ordered by mail from the publisher.
Please include $2.50 for postage and handling.
But try your bookstore first!

This edition published by Running Press Kids, an imprint of
Running Press Book Publishers
2300 Chestnut Street, Suite 200
Philadelphia, PA 19103-4371

Visit us on the web!
www.runningpress.com

Ages 7–10
Grades 2–4

CHAPTER 1

I'm scared of bunny rabbits.

Yes, it's true. I'm really, really
scared of them. Bunny rabbits are soft
and fluffy and round and small and . . .

Really, really BAD.

They've got SCARY little bunny
faces and long NASTY bunny ears and
they stare at you with those EVIL
bunny eyes, and they wiggle and they
twitch and they stick out those

DEADLY bunny teeth. . . . They give me nightmares, they make me freak out. I just need to think of one and my hands go shaky, my skin goes shivery, my heart starts going POPPA POPPA POPPA like a popcorn machine.

I know it's stupid to be scared of bunnies. I mean, I'm a big, tough nine-year-old girl who isn't scared of anything much.

I'm not scared of spiders. My mother is terrified of spiders. If she sees a spider in the house, she starts flapping her arms around, screaming, "GET RID OF IT, SANDRA, GET RID OF IT!" until I pick it up on a piece of

paper and carry it outside. Then Mom
makes me throw away the piece of
paper, wash my hands twice, and then
she locks the door, just in case the
spider somehow works out how to use
a door handle.

I'm not scared of swimming in deep water either. My grandpop hates swimming in deep water. You see, he hasn't got very good eyesight. If we go swimming in the sea together, he sees shadows in the water and he starts

freaking out, yelling, "WHAT'S THAT DOWN THERE, SANDRA, I SEE SOMETHING MOVING DOWN THERE, TELL ME WHAT IT IS, SANDRA!" And I'll say, "Grandpop, it's just your feet, you're looking at your own feet," and he'll freak out even more and say, "DID YOU SAY IT'S GOT TEETH? WHAT'S GOT TEETH? TELL ME, SANDRA, WHAT'S GOT TEETH?" Grandpop hasn't got very good hearing either.

But I'm not scared of stuff like that. I'm not scared of dentists or snakes or heights or bugs or frogs or clowns or jellyfish or fire or storms or loud noises

or small spaces or big crowds or flying
in planes or riding on skateboards or
watching scary movies or sleeping in
the dark. My little brother is SOOOOO
scared of the dark, he sleeps with all
the lights on and the door wide open.

He doesn't even like closing his eyes. If we ever have to go out somewhere at night, like to a party or to a movie or for a walk, he won't step out of the house without taking a flashlight with him—and a packet of spare batteries, just in case.

CHAPTER 2

So everyone has some kind of fear,
and mine just happens to be bunnies.
I have no idea how it all started.
Maybe it's just one of those ridiculous
little fears that has no reason at all.
Or maybe, just maybe, it has something to do with when I was little and
Grandpop gave me a pet bunny. He
didn't get it from a pet store. He found
it on the side of the road after it'd been

hit by a car and it was all covered with dirt and grass and bugs.

He said, "Here Sandra, why don't you take care of this little bunny?"

When he gave it to me, it bit me on the hand, jumped out of my arms, then

ran into the laundry room where it got stuck behind the water heater. We couldn't get it out, not with the broom handle, not with the barbecue tongs, not with a coat hanger.

Then Mom had this brilliant idea of turning on the vacuum cleaner, sticking the nozzle behind the water heater, and trying to gently suck up the bunny because she'd seen a vacuum cleaner ad on TV where a guy lifted up a bowling ball with a vacuum cleaner—and she thought it might work on a bunny too. But the bunny didn't suck up. Its ears just flapped around in the nozzle, FLUPPA

FLUPPA FLUPPA. It stayed there for the rest of the day until a man came to our house and got it out with a special hook on a long stick. He took the bunny away in a van and we never saw it again.

But like I said, my fear of bunnies probably has no reason at all.

All I know is, life becomes a little tricky if you need to avoid bunnies all the time. There seem to be a lot of bunnies around the place. I can't visit my friend Lily because she has a pet bunny in her backyard. And I couldn't see the school holiday magic show because the magician does a trick where he pulls a bunny out of his hat. I can't watch kids' shows on TV, because just about every kids' show has a bunny in it somewhere. When my brother watches TV, I have to sit with Grandpop and watch baseball on

his little TV in his bedroom, which is
pretty boring. At least I'm sure that no
bunnies will ever play baseball.

I've kept my life as bunny-free as
possible, but sometimes you can't avoid
a bunny incident here and there,

especially when you have a stupid little brother like my brother Hamish. He's three years younger than me and he's a big bully. A big bunny bully. He's always making some kind of stupid joke about how I'm scared of bunnies.

Or he hides a picture of a bunny under my pillow so I find it when I go to bed. Sometimes his little friend PJ sleeps over and they follow me around all weekend making bunny noises and twitching their noses in a bunny-ish way, saying "Oooo, watch out, a bunny's gonna get you . . . watch out, Sandra, ha ha ha ha." I know it's crazy, but it really freaks me out.

One time they crept up outside my bedroom window and held up two big bunny ears and chanted, "Here comes da bunny . . . da big bad bunny!" I knew the ears were just cardboard, and I knew it was just my stupid little

brother and his stupid little friend, but
still, it really was . . .

Scary.

There are other times you can have
an unexpected bunny situation. You

can be having a perfectly nice day and, out of nowhere, a bunny can just spring itself on you without you ever expecting it. And that's what happened to me just the other day, on a Saturday morning, when Mom and Grandpop took me and my brother to a carnival in the city. . . .

CHAPTER 3

At first everything was going really well. All around me were rides and games and food stands and I wanted to do EVERYTHING.

First, I wanted to go on the Super Slide. It's this enormous slide with a whole bunch of big bumps that make it really fun to go down. Mom wasn't so sure about it. She said the bumps could give you twelve different kinds of neck injuries. Nobody wanted to go on

the Super Slide with me. Mom said,
"No way" and Grandpop said, "Not a
chance" and my little brother Hamish
didn't say anything. He just stared up
at the slide and I knew he was scared
because the hair was standing up on

the back of his neck and his arms and his legs—he's a pretty hairy kid.

I said, "You are such a scaredy, Hamish, it's nothing, it's just a slide. Come on, someone go with me, please, please, PLEASE?" and I put on my saddest, cutest face.

Eventually Grandpop said, "All right, Sandra, I'll go on it with you, come on."

He bought some tickets and we walked up a whole bunch of stairs. Grandpop was already looking frightened. He said, "It's pretty high up here, Sandra . . . it's not too late to change your mind."

But I wasn't going to change my
mind, it looked like too much fun.
When we got to the top, a man gave us
slippery sacks that you sit on to make
the ride go faster. I sat on my sack and
I went down, really fast, over a bump,
over a bump, over a bump, all the way

to the bottom. WHOOOO HOOOOO! It was great, the best ride ever. Then it was Grandpop's turn. He came down really slow, because he decided not to

sit on his slippery sack. Instead, he held the sack out in front of him, just in case he started feeling sick on the way down.

Okay, we'd done the Super Slide; now I wanted to go on something even SCARIER. I saw a whole bunch of people standing in a line waiting to go on the Tunnel of Terror—a really spooky train ride into a dark tunnel full of ghosts and skeletons and monsters.

I said, "C'mon everyone, let's go on the Tunnel of Terror," and Mom said, "No, I don't really like those spooky rides." Grandpop said, "Sorry, Sandra,

I think I need to rest for a bit," because he was still feeling funny after the Super Slide. And Hamish didn't say anything. He just shook his head slowly, because he knew it was going to be dark in the Tunnel of Terror and he'd forgotten to bring his flashlight.

I said, "Ha ha, look at you Hamish, you're such a baby, it's just a little ride, somebody go on with me, please, please, PLEASE?" and I put on my most adorable, I'm-so-disappointed face.

Mom said, "All right, Sandra, I guess I'll go with you, it can't be THAT scary."

So Mom and I got in the line for
the Tunnel of Terror and I said, "This
is going to be so cool, Mom. There's a
dangly skeleton that jumps out in
front of you and rubber things that
flap in your face, and a bony hand

that reaches out and taps you on
the shoulder."

Mom started laughing and going,
"Ooooo, I'm so scared, ha ha ha ha, I'm
so scared," and then a bony hand

reached out and tapped Mom on the shoulder and she screamed, "YAHHHHHHHH!" It was just the woman standing behind us in the line. She wanted to know where to buy the tickets for the ride, but it really freaked out poor Mom. Mom told the woman to try the ticket booth around the corner. She stayed pretty quiet after that, and when we finally got on the ride she just sat there with her hands over her eyes, which was lucky, because I don't think she would've liked the giant spider with giant fangs and furry legs and big red flashing eyes that fell down from the ceiling on a long web and hung right over her.

After the Tunnel of Terror I was getting hungry, so I said, "Can we get something to eat, can we, can we?"

Grandpop said, "Sure, let's go to that nice little health food stand and get a sandwich and some fresh orange juice," but I didn't want a sandwich and orange juice, that sounded so boring. I wanted to eat something a little bit more exciting. I wanted something from the old greasy food trailer that was parked right NEXT to the nice little health food stand. There was a big rusty sign out the front that said you could buy chili dogs, and

burgers, and deep-fried frankfurters
dipped in yellow batter. Everyone was
too scared to eat this stuff. Mom just
made a disgusted face and said, "Not
for me." Grandpop just gulped and

said, "Umm, I don't think so," and Hamish didn't say anything. He couldn't speak because he was holding his hand over his nose and mouth, trying not to breathe in the smell of bubbling bacon fat.

But I wasn't scared. I said, "Look at Hamish, ha ha, he's even scared of food. Well, I'm not scared, can I buy some? Please, please, PLEASE?" and I put on my cutest, sweetest, don't-you-love-me-any-more face. Grandpop gave me four dollars and I bought myself a double foot-long chili hot dog with mustard and pickles and fried onions and grated cheese. I ate it in front of

Mom and Grandpop and Hamish, ate
every last bit, licked my fingers, then
washed the whole thing down with a
raspberry and lime super-slurpee, with
a dollop of extra caramel fudge.

What next, what next? There were
so many things I wanted to do. But
just then Hamish spotted something
that HE wanted to do. It was way
across on the other side of the carnival,

past the really cool Gravitron ride
where you spin round and round until
your hair stands up, beyond the
amazing Death-Drop where you get
lifted up into the sky really high and
dropped down really fast, just a bit
further than the brilliant Pirate Ship
where you get rocked back and forth
and you think you're going to go
upside-down. . . .

It was the Itty Bitty Petting Zoo.

CHAPTER 4

In a quiet little corner of the carnival was a fenced-off area where you could sit and pat cute farmyard animals for as long as you liked. This was Hamish's idea of fun, but not MY idea of fun, because in an Itty Bitty Petting Zoo, there might be . . .

An itty bitty bunny.

Hamish said, "Can we go to the Petting Zoo?" and Mom said, "Of course, Hamish, that looks like a really good thing for the whole family to do."

I wasn't happy at all. I said, "No Mom, I don't want to go in there. They might have . . . bunnies."

Mom said, "Oh Sandra, you're being ridiculous. You've got to get over this silly rabbit thing. Rabbits don't hurt, they're soft and round and fluffy and cute. And anyway, we've been doing everything YOU'VE wanted to do, even though some of those things have really scared us, so now I think it's time for you to do something that WE want to do."

I said, "Please, Mom, no, no."

Hamish said, "Look at Sandra, she's a little scaredy baby. I mean, it's just a petting zoo, ha ha ha." Then he gave Mom and Grandpop his biggest, most adorable smiley face and said in

his sweetest little kiddie voice, "I
WANT TO GO TO THE ITTY BITTY
PETTING ZOO, I WANT TO GO NOW,
NOW, NOWWWWWWWWW." Froth

was coming out of his mouth so Mom and Grandpop thought they'd better take him.

My hands went sweaty, my skin went shivery. We walked slowly toward that Petting Zoo and my heart was doing the POPPA POPPA POPPA popcorn-machine thing. Mom bought four tickets. We walked in through a big squeaky gate. . . .

And then I was inside. Standing on straw. Breathing in the smell of fur and food and poo. . . .

Maybe even . . . BUNNY poo.

Kids and parents were all around, patting the animals. I saw a calf and a couple of goats and a whole bunch of quacking ducks and a little spotted piglet that ran around and around. All

the kids were trying to pat it, saying,
"It's soooooo cute, it's soooo cute." Until
it peed down its own leg and then
nobody wanted to pat it any more.

I stayed beside the fence, right next
to the gate, in case I needed to make a
quick escape. I couldn't see any

bunnies, but I knew they were in there
. . . hiding somewhere. Maybe they
were creeping behind the feed bucket,
maybe they were lurking in the deep
straw. They were waiting for me with
their SCARY little bunny faces and
their long EVIL bunny ears and their
NASTY wet pink little bunny noses.

Hamish was having a great time.
He'd dragged Mom and Grandpop off
to see the guinea pigs. I saw him
picking them up by the ears and
squeezing them around the neck and
dropping them on their heads. He just
loves guinea pigs. But me, I didn't
budge. I huddled beside that fence,

right next to a little baby chicken, both of us trembling. Nearby, there was a little girl and her Mom. The little girl pointed at me, saying, "Look Mommy, I see a chicken over there, I see a little chicken."

I thought she was talking about me so I yelled back, "I'm not a little chicken! I'm not. I'm not scared of anything in the whole world, except for bunnies, okay, SO DON'T CALL ME A LITTLE CHICKEN." The little girl and her mom left me pretty much alone after that.

After a few minutes, my arms started getting a bit sore. I had wire

marks on the back of my elbows from
pressing so hard against that fence.
Maybe I should step away, try patting
an animal or two. I peered around: no
bunnies anywhere, it was safe. With

eyes focused and senses alert, I walked towards the middle of the Petting Zoo. One step, two steps, two-and-a-half steps. I went up to the calf and gave it

a pat. It had a nice face and its fur was all hard and smooth. Then I went over to the little goat and touched the horn on top of its head. The horn felt long and rough and really weird. Hey, this wasn't too bad, not bad at all. I went over to the grain bucket and got a bit of grain and held it out for a lamb to eat. The lamb wasn't interested in it, but a two-year-old kid came over and licked it right out of my hand.

This was turning out to be fun. I even thought the geese were kind of cute. I liked how they flapped their wings and chased the little kids around, making horrible honking

noises. Hamish was so scared of the
geese, he kept running away from
them. I yelled out, "Ha ha, look at you
Hamish, you're a big goose who's
scared of geese, ha ha." I reached down
to show him that I was brave enough

to pat a goose . . . and that's when I felt
something brushing against the back
of my leg.

A soft, fluffy something.

CHAPTER 5

I froze. A couple of kids looked over
at whatever it was that was brushing
against the back of my leg and
they said, "Awwwwwww, look at that,
so cute."

Then, whatever it was suddenly
moved.

A floppy ear brushed my leg and a
wet nose rubbed against me.
Immediately my stomach flipped and
flipped again. That double foot-long

chili hot dog with mustard and pickles
and onions and grated cheese started
doing a gymnastics session in my gut.
I thought to myself, don't look down
Sandra, don't look down, don't look
down, don't look down, don't look

down, don't look down, don't look
down, don't look down, don't look
down, DON'T LOOK DOWN, DON'T
LOOK DOWN, DON'T LOOK DOWN,
DON'T LOOK DOWN, DON'T
LOOK DOWN. . . .

I looked down.

It was lurking behind my left leg.
A nose-twitching, eyelash-batting,
cotton-tailed BIG BAD BUNNY.

It started nuzzling me with its
GREAT MENACING JAWS and
it looked up at me with its MEAN
HARD FACE and it wriggled its
SHARP DEADLY EARS and then . . .
and then . . .

Oh no.

It hippity-hopped onto my foot.

IT ACTUALLY HIPPITY-HOPPED
RIGHT ONTO MY FOOT and just sat
there on my shoe, doing nothing.

All the kids in the whole petting zoo
came over to see this amazing bunny

sight, including all the parents, the animal keeper, the ticket-seller, my mom, my grandpop, and my stupid little brother Hamish. Everyone was smiling and staring at that bunny, going, "Awwwwwwww, look at that, it's on her foot, so cute."

I couldn't move, couldn't breathe. I just stood there, waiting for it to attack, waiting for this rabid rabbit to rip off my leg with its deadly fangs, waiting for my life to end in a most gruesome mangled way. Tomorrow, all the newspapers in the world would have a great gory headline slashed across the front page: "BIG BAD

BUNNY STRIKES! NINE-YEAR-OLD
GIRL NIBBLED TO PIECES!" There'd
be a photo of me—or at least whatever

bits of me were left. My mom and grandpop would be looking on with sad faces, and Hamish would be standing there, pointing and laughing.

I waited and waited and waited for that bunny to strike.

But nothing. No biting. No nibbling. No eating. No tragedy.

It actually seemed quite . . . harmless.

Kind of . . . quiet.

Kind of . . . almost . . .

Friendly.

CHAPTER 6

The kids in the Petting Zoo started chanting, "Pick it up, pick it up!"

I thought to myself, "Okay, maybe this is it, maybe the time has finally come to confront my fear once and for all. I mean, it's just a harmless little bunny."

Taking a deep breath, I reached down. Slowly, closer. My hand was almost within reach of its little bunny head. And then . . .

In one move, I whacked it off my foot, just whacked that horrible little thing right off my shoe. It flew through the air, bounced off the side of a sheep,

fell into some soft hay, then it hippity-
hopped to the other side of the Itty
Bitty Petting Zoo, as far away from me
as possible.

Everyone stared—all the kids, the
parents, the animal keeper, the ticket-
seller, my mom, my grandpop, my

stupid little brother Hamish. I had
to get out of that Petting Zoo, fast. I
took off for the gate, running. I didn't
care what was in my way, what I
was stepping on. If it squeaked, it was
probably a duck, if it squealed it
was probably a pig, if it shrieked, it
was probably a kid. I got out of there,
slammed the gate shut, and stood, all
hunched over, puffing like mad,
desperately trying to rub the bunny
germs off my shoe with an old ice-
cream wrapper. I was going to be okay,
it was over, all over. . . .

Then I looked up.

Standing in front of me was . . .

A GIGANTIC BLUE AND YELLOW POLKA-DOTTED BUNNY with huge ears and a massive nose and horrible creepy fangs.

ARGGGGGGGHHHHH!

It came up to me, patted my head, and said, "Don't look sad, little girl. Barton the Bunny will cheer you up!"

It was a person inside a bunny suit. He put a pair of Barton the Bunny ears on my head and a Barton the Bunny nose on my face and handed me an enormous blue and yellow polka-dotted Barton the Bunny balloon. Finally, he gave me a BIG Barton the Bunny hug and hippity-hopped away.

From behind me, in the petting
zoo, I heard a giggle. It was Hamish.
Then other people started chuckling,
then there were more giggles and
more chuckles, and soon everyone in

the entire petting zoo was pointing at me and laughing, laughing and pointing. . . .

No one said a thing on the way home in the car. There wasn't much to say. Hamish was still giggling, and I kept saying, "Stop it, Hamish, stop it," but deep down inside I knew he had good reason to giggle. I was an embarrassment to the family—a bunny-hating embarrassment, squished up beside an enormous blue and yellow polka-dotted Barton the Bunny balloon.

(HAPTER 7

The sad fact is, I don't think I'm ever
going to like bunnies. But that Petting
Zoo experience wasn't a complete
waste of time. Now at least I know
that they're not going to kill me. And
maybe, just maybe, I can start trying
to deal with them. Maybe I'll have the
guts now to watch a Bugs Bunny
cartoon. One day I might be able to see
a magician pull a bunny out of his hat.
Or if I really work hard at it, maybe,

just maybe, one day I might be able to actually . . . touch one. Without whacking it.

Another good thing came out of the Itty Bitty Petting Zoo: I finally worked out a way of getting back at my stupid little brother. Next weekend I'm going to walk past his bedroom window and I'm going to hold up a gigantic cardboard cut-out of a goose.

And I'm going to do it at night.

From Danny Katz

I think I was around eight years old when Dad took us all on a trip to an outback mining town called Broken Hill. I don't know why he took us there, but he's a geologist, he's really into rocks, so maybe he wanted to go to Broken Hill to see if he could fix it. Anyway, on the way there, he spotted a rabbit on the side of the road—it'd been hit by a car—so Dad pulled over to see if it was all right. Turns out this rabbit wasn't well at all; it was twitchy and all swollen and it had a rabbit disease called myxomatosis which made its eyes gooey. And because Dad is such a kind, caring kind of guy, he decided to help this sick rabbit, BY PUTTING IT IN THE CAR, MAKING ME HOLD IT ON MY LAP, AND DRIVING FOR THREE-AND-A-HALF HOURS TO THE NEAREST VET.

So that's how it started, my fear of bunnies. I'm forty-two, and I still haven't really gotten over it.

From Mitch Vane

When we were kids, my sister Becky had an albino rabbit as a pet. It was pretty cute, as most bunnies are, but it had these big, spooky red eyes, which kind of freaked me out. I didn't go near it that much, but I did feel sad when it came to a rather grizzly end in the backyard.

All these years later, my sister still has rabbits as pets, but I will always remember her first, slightly evil-looking bunny. I tapped into these memories when I came to draw the characters in this book—I really related to Sandra's fear and had no problem drawing rabbits that looked cute . . . but just a little menacing.